HELEN MOR

SATCHKIN PATCHKIN

ILLUSTRATED BY
SHIRLEY HUGHES

PUFFIN BOOKS
IN ASSOCIATION WITH
FABER & FABER

Puffin Books, Penguin Books Ltd, 27 Wrights Lane, London W8 5TZ (Publishing and Editorial)
and Harmondsworth, Middlesex, England (Distribution and Warehouse)
Viking Penguin Inc., 40 West 23rd Street, New York, New York 10010, U.S.A.
Penguin Books Australia Ltd, Ringwood, Victoria, Australia
Penguin Books Canada Ltd, 2801 John Street, Markham, Ontario, Canada L3R 1B4
Penguin Books (N.Z.) Ltd, 182–190 Wairau Road, Auckland 10, New Zealand

—

First published by Faber & Faber 1966
Published in Puffin Books 1978
Reprinted 1986

—

Copyright © Helen Morgan, 1966
Illustrations copyright © Faber & Faber Ltd, 1966
All rights reserved

—

Made and printed in Great Britain by
Richard Clay Ltd, Bungay, Suffolk
Set in Monotype Bembo

PUFFIN BOOKS

SATCHKIN PATCHKIN

'Seventeen cows in the byre,' said the little green magic man as he turned away from the greedy farmer's locked and bolted door, 'and not a mouthful of milk to spare for a stranger,' and he drifted back across the clovery fields to the small untidy cottage where lived a poor widow called Mother Farthing.

He banged on the old woman's door, and, sure enough, she poured the last drops of milk she had into a thimble, and gave them to him. She was kinder than the farmer, for all she was so poor, and the magic man liked her for it.

'If ever you need me,' he said, 'you have only to come and call. My name is Satchkin Patchkin and I live, like a leaf, in the apple tree.'

So the little old woman and Satchkin Patchkin, the little green magic man, became friends. She shared her baking and was kind to him, and he used his magic to help her, especially when the greedy farmer, who was also her landlord, came worrying her with all his demands. Was it her chickens he wanted, or her apples and blackberries? – Satchkin Patchkin would soon see about that, and, what was more, he would see that he made her more prosperous and happy than she had been for years!

Helen Morgan was born in 1921 and became a bookworm as soon as she could read. By the time she was fifteen she had written two novels, but her father burnt them because she was so bad at her school subjects, except English and cooking. She is married with three daughters.

CONTENTS

I

WHO WILL
LIFT THE LATCH?

ONCE UPON a time there was a little green magic man. His name was Satchkin Patchkin and he lived, like a leaf, in an apple tree.

The apple tree grew by the hedge at the bottom of a long, untidy garden. At the other end of the long, untidy garden was a small untidy cottage.

A poor widow woman called Mother Farthing lived in the cottage, but it did not belong to her. It belonged to the farmer who lived in the house on the hill. He was a lean man, a mean man, a man without a smile.

One sweet spring night, when the dew was deep, Mother Farthing came walking late down the lane.

She had been to the market to sell her one good cow. Her feet were slow and her heart was sad as she came to her cottage alone.

'My cow is gone,' she sighed when she reached the gate. The gold in her purse was no comfort. The poor woman needed it all to pay the farmer his rent.

In the clear, pale sky, beyond the hedge, the round, white moon was rising. The old woman watched it, her hand on the latch of her cottage door.

'I looked on the moon as a lantern,' she said, 'to save me the cost of a candle. But tonight I see it is more like a bowl of milk.'

The little green magic man in the apple tree heard her. He came out from among the new young leaves and looked at the moon for himself.

'Milk,' he said, thoughtfully, staring up at the sky. 'How many moons have grown fat and grown thin since I last took a drink of milk? It is so long ago I have quite forgotten the taste.'

The more he pondered and the more he wondered the more he wanted milk. He told himself that milk he must have or sleep he would have none.

By way of the garden he went, and by way of the lane, with feet as light and fleet as a hurrying hare. Then under a five-barred gate he skipped and over a clovery field to the edge of a stream.

Across the dimpling water leapt the little green magic man, twisting and turning, swift as a leaf in a gale.

High on the hill-top the farmer's fine house was in darkness. Under his quilted counterpane, warm in his feather bed, the farmer was fast asleep.

Into his dreams, that were always full of money, came the sound of banging and shouting.

Waking and shaking his head, the farmer sat up, knuckling his sleepy eyes.

Beside him, buried in blankets, his wife was still asleep. He woke her up at once.

'What's all that noise?' she grumbled. 'What's all that banging and shouting down in the yard?'

'How should I know?' snapped the farmer. 'I have hardly had time to wake up.'

'Time enough to waken *me*,' snapped his wife. 'Open the window and see who is down below.'

The farmer climbed, muttering, out of his warm, soft bed and went to open the window. In the shivering draught he shouted down to the shadows.

'Who's there? And what do you want at this time of night?'

Back came the answer, thin and clear as the ring of a silver bell.

'Satchkin Patchkin!
Who will lift the latchkin?
Satchkin Patchkin!
Who will lift the latch?'

The farmer leaned out of the window, but he could see no one down by the door, in spite of the light the moon had spilled on the steps.

'What do you want?' he bellowed, angry at being kept out of bed in the cold.

'A mouthful of milk,' said the clear, thin voice from below. 'Only a mouthful of milk, that's all.'

'Milk!' roared the farmer. 'Milk! At this time of night? Be off with you now, whoever you are and let me get back to my bed!'

He slammed the window shut and went, shivering, back to the waiting warmth of his bed.

The little green magic man turned away from the locked and bolted door. 'Seventeen cows in the byre,' he said, 'and not a mouthful of milk to spare for a stranger.'

Slowly, now, he went back the way he had come, drifting across the stream like a dragon-fly, crossing the clovery fields to the five-barred gate and the lane.

When he reached Mother Farthing's small, untidy cottage he stopped.

'I *must* have a mouthful of milk,' he said to himself. 'Trying to remember the taste will torment me all night.'

He began to bang on the old woman's door.

Mother Farthing was lying awake in her narrow bed, mourning the loss of her cow. She got up at once and went to the window.

'Who's there?' she called. 'What can I do for you?'

The answer came thin and clear, like the sound of a silver bell.

> 'Satchkin Patchkin!
> Will you lift the latchkin?
> Satchkin Patchkin!
> Will you lift the latch?'

'Of course I will!' cried the old woman. 'I'll come down at once.'

Down the crooked stairs she went, feeling her way

in the darkness. Her feet were bare and the great square flags of the kitchen floor were cold.

'I'm coming!' she called as she hurried towards the door.

She lifted the latch and the creaking door swung open. Only the moonlight came in, silent and bright, lighting the poor, shabby kitchen better than any candle.

'Who's there?' called Mother Farthing. 'Who knocked? What is it you want?'

'A mouthful of milk,' said a clear, thin voice behind her. 'A mouthful of milk, nothing more.'

The old woman turned and looked about her. 'Who is it?' she asked. 'Where are you hiding yourself?'

'I am here on your table,' said the voice. 'Look closely and you will see.'

So she looked – and she saw a little green magic man.

'Mercy on us!' she cried. 'How did you get up there?'

'The draught from the door blew me up,' answered Satchkin Patchkin. 'Will you give me a mouthful of milk?'

Poor Mother Farthing sat down and wept.

'I have sold my one cow,' she sobbed. 'I drank the last of her milk for my supper. There was nothing else in the house.'

'Is it *all* gone?' asked the little green magic man. 'Every last drop of it?'

The old woman stood up and lifted the jug from the dresser. 'One drop,' she said, tilting it sideways. 'No more than enough to fill a thimble, I fear.'

'A thimbleful is enough for me!' cried Satchkin Patchkin.

So Mother Farthing fetched her silver thimble and drained into it the last of the milk from the jug. Then she gave it to the little green magic man.

He drank it slowly, remembering how it tasted. When he had finished, he flung the thimble high in the air. It dropped, clattering, into the jug.

At once the jug was full of sweet, new milk.

'You will never again want for milk,' said Satchkin Patchkin. 'Throw your thimble into the jug, open the door and say:

> "Satchkin Patchkin,
> Hear me lift the latchkin.
> Satchkin Patchkin,
> Hear me lift the latch"

and the jug will be filled with milk.'

'Thank you,' said Mother Farthing. 'I shan't forget your kindness.'

The little green magic man sprang from the table on to the silver path the moon had put down by the door. 'If ever you need me,' he said, drifting into the garden, 'you have only to come and call. My name is Satchkin Patchkin and I live, like a leaf, in the apple tree.'

2

WHO WILL
MEND THE THATCH?

ONCE UPON a time there was a little green magic
man. His name was Satchkin Patchkin and he lived,
like a leaf, in an apple tree.

The apple tree grew by the hedge at the bottom of
a long, untidy garden. At the other end of the long,
untidy garden was the small, untidy cottage where
Mother Farthing lived. Its windows were cracked, its
doors hung askew and the thatch on its tip-tilted
roof needed mending.

One wild night, one wet night, poor Mother
Farthing lay in her narrow bed listening to the rain
dripping in through the roof and the wind whistling
in through the windows.

'If only I had had a little more gold when my cow
was sold,' she thought, 'I could at least have had the
leaking roof repaired.'

All about the bedroom floor were buckets and
bowls. The old woman had put them there to catch

the water that dripped and splashed and streamed through the tattered thatch.

'I must do something about the draught,' she thought, shivering under her blankets. The wild wind whistled in through the cracks in the casement, billowing the faded curtains, rattling the bedroom door. Mother Farthing climbed out of bed, picked up the old rag rug from the floor and went towards the window.

As she struggled to hang the rug on the hooks in the frame, she saw in the half-light the windy waste of her long, untidy garden. Dark in the dark above the hedge, rose the tossed and tormented shape of the apple tree.

'Dear me!' cried the old woman, forgetting the rug and the rain and the rattling, chattering cold. 'The little green magic man must be having a terrible time out there tonight!'

She snatched up a blanket from the bed, flung it about her shoulders and stumbled her way down the crooked stairs to the kitchen.

As she drew the bolt on the big, ill-fitting back door the wind came roaring in, sending the poor woman staggering, in a scatter of chilly rain.

She clung to the door handle, crying into the night:

> 'Satchkin Patchkin,
> Hear me lift the latchkin!
> Satchkin Patchkin,
> Hear me lift the latch!'

There was a sudden silence and out of the silence a voice like the sound of a far-off bell said, 'You have forgotten to throw the thimble into the jug.'

'It was not milk I wanted,' answered Mother Farthing. 'I was going to ask you to come into the chimney corner for the night. I saw your tree bent by the wind and thought how cold you must be.'

'That was a kindly thought,' said the little green magic man, flitting like a moth from floor to table. 'I was snug enough, though, curled up in a crack in the trunk, well away from the wind.'

'You were better off than I was, then,' sighed the old woman. 'My roof leaks and my room is full of rain.'

'Will your landlord not repair it?' asked Satchkin Patchkin.

'No,' said the old woman. 'He is a lean man, a mean man, a man without a smile. He takes his rent and does nothing for his tenants.'

'Leave him to me,' said the little green magic man. 'Go back to your bed and hide your head and try to sleep a little.'

Then he was gone and with his going the silence went out of the night and the wind and the rain returned.

Back in her damp and draughty room the old woman covered her head with the bedclothes and shut her eyes for sleep.

Out in the darkness the little green magic man flashed like a spear of lightning to the farmhouse high on the hill.

He banged on the stout oak door like the drums of thunder.

'Who's there?' roared the farmer, rolling out of the feathery depths of his bed. He went to the window and pressed his face against the rain-streaked glass.

There was a sudden silence and out of the silence a voice like a faint, far bell called, clearly:

> 'Satchkin Patchkin
> Who will mend the thatchkin?
> Satchkin Patchkin!
> Who will mend the thatch?'

'What thatch?' bellowed the farmer.

'Mother Farthing's thatch,' came the answer. 'Her cottage is leaking and creaking and lets in the wind and the rain.'

The farmer thumped his fist angrily on the windowsill. 'What care I for the wind and the rain in an old woman's tumbledown cottage?' he cried. 'Tell her that she must mend the roof herself. Be off with you, now – and let me get back to my bed.'

Away went the little green magic man and away went the spell of silence. The wind howled again and a flurry of rain beat at the farmhouse windows.

Grunting and grumbling the farmer went stumbling back to his silk-quilted bed. His wife stirred in her sleep, pulling her pillow down into the hollow she had made in the feather-filled mattress. She slept deep, she slept warm. She did not hear the storm.

In her narrow bed, under her shabby blankets, Mother Farthing was not asleep. She heard the storm begin again after the strange, small silence and she knew it had something to do with the little green magic man.

'What mysteries is he at, now?' she wondered. 'What spell has he put on the night?'

Hardly had the thought come into her head when the room was filled with light. A white light, a bright

light, that shone in every corner. It showed the old woman the rain coming in through the roof in a dozen different places. Then the light went out and the voice of Satchkin Patchkin said, close to her ear:

> 'Satchkin Patchkin,
> I will mend the thatchkin.
> Satchkin Patchkin,
> I will mend the thatch!'

At once there was a tearing and a roaring and all the old thatch went soaring up into the sky. The old woman shrieked and covered her face with the pillow.

'Have no fear,' said the little green magic man softly. 'You will come to no harm, I promise you.'

At this, the old woman took the pillow away from her face. Through the rafters above her head she could see the sky. It was cloudless and clear and full of splendid stars. The rain had stopped and the wind had died down to a whisper.

The little green magic man leapt from the bed and drifted, frail as a feather, on to the windowsill. He turned himself round and around on the breath of the wind and cried:

> 'Satchkin Patchkin,
> Come and mend the thatchkin!
> Satchkin Patchkin,
> Come and mend the thatch!'

In the grass, in the leaves, the wind began to move. Over the meadows and through the woods, up the hill and into the farmyard it blew. From the barns, from the sheds, from the cows' very beds, it swept up the strands of straw. A stack toppled and fell, straw streamed down the hill in the wind that was turning round.

The old woman, watching the sky, saw the straw cloud coming and sat up in bed with a cry of surprise.

She watched as the wind took the straw stem by

stem and set it straight. Then, threading and winding and twisting and binding itself, the straw took the shape of a roof.

High in the sky it hung for a moment, shimmering under the stars. Then it came down on the rafters with no more noise than a counterpane covering a bed.

With a last little sigh the wind rustled into the grass.

'Sleep well,' said the little green magic man from the windowsill. Then he stepped through a broken pane and drifted into the garden.

As she slipped into sleep the old woman thought she could still hear him calling. From a long way away he seemed to say, 'My name is Satchkin Patchkin and I live, like a leaf, in the apple tree.'

3

YOUR HENS
YOU SHALL NOT SNATCH

ONCE UPON a time there was a little green magic man. His name was Satchkin Patchkin and he lived, like a leaf, in an apple tree.

The apple tree grew by the hedge at the bottom of a long, untidy garden. At the other end of the long, untidy garden was the small, untidy cottage where Mother Farthing lived. Its windows were cracked and its doors hung askew, but the thatch on its tip-tilted roof was new.

One balmy, blue-and-white morning when the apple tree was rosy with blossom, the old woman stood in her long, untidy garden and looked up at her small, untidy cottage.

'Now that I have a new roof,' she said to herself, 'I must find a way to get the windows mended.'

In the grass by the hedge seven hens were scratching about. Three were brown and three were white and one was small and black as night.

'Useless creatures,' sighed Mother Farthing. 'They have not laid me an egg for days. I will take them to market and see what pence I can get for them.'

She fetched an old wickerwork hamper from the outhouse and set it down by the gate. One by one she chased and caught the hens, shutting each struggling, squawking, flappity, feather-shedding bird into the basket before she went back for the next.

At last they were all safely in – all save the little black hen. She was under the hedge down by the apple tree.

Quietly the old woman moved through the long grass towards the bird, thinking she might be able to take her by surprise. With her feathers well smoothed and her small feet well tucked the little black hen sat quite still and clucked.

The old woman crept closer and closer through the rustling tussocks of grass. When she was near enough, she leapt at the hen, hoping to snatch her and catch her. With a squawk and a scurry, in a flurry of hurrying feathers, the frightened bird flew into the apple tree.

A shower of blossoms snowed over the old woman's shawl. She cried out to the little green magic man she knew was above in the leaves:

'Satchkin Patchkin!
My hen I cannot snatchkin!
Satchkin Patchkin,
My hen I cannot snatch!'

'Leave her to me,' said a voice as cool and clear as a drop of spring water. 'Be off with you, now, to the market.'

So the old woman walked away up the long, untidy garden, her worn shoes trampling the unkempt grass, pale blossoms blowing down from her shabby shawl.

She put on her bonnet and tied her purse round her waist. Then, with a snap and a strong leather strap, she fastened the wickerwork basket. She heaved it on to her shoulders and began the long slow climb up the lane to the town that was over the hill.

The busy day was half done by the time Mother Farthing trudged into the market square. She was tired, she was stumbling, her hair was all tumbling and her bonnet was awry. She found a space in a small dark place and sat down to call her wares.

No one wanted the hens in her basket. Jostling and bustling, the crowd hurried by, not heeding, not hearing, her thin, tired cry.

It grew late. The square emptied. The noise of the day died away. With a sigh the old woman stood up and lifted the heavy hamper once more to her aching shoulder.

A man came suddenly out of a cheerful tavern. His eyes were not looking the way that his feet were walking and he bumped himself hard on the old woman's cumbersome burden. He staggered and grumbled, she staggered and stumbled and fell in a heap in the mire.

'Get out of my way, old woman,' shouted the man. He was a lean man, a mean man, a man without a smile – the old woman's landlord, the farmer who lived on the hill.

Mother Farthing was trying to wipe the mud from her skirts. As soon as she lifted her head he knew her and said, 'So it's you, Mother Farthing. And what are you selling, pray? Nothing worth having, I'll be bound!'

'No,' said a voice like a splinter of ice. 'Nothing worth having or *you* would have had it long ago!'

The farmer heard it and his face went red with rage.

The old woman heard it and knew it was Satchkin Patchkin.

'Open your hamper, old woman,' commanded the farmer. 'Let me look at your wares.'

The old woman stuttered and mumbled and muttered, unwilling to open the basket. She knew that the farmer would have her hens and not give her what they were worth.

A cheapjack, clearing his stall, came to help Mother Farthing.

'Six fine hens!' he cried, opening the basket. 'Six beautiful hens, each worth its weight in gold!'

'A likely tale!' snorted the lean, mean man. 'Six skinny draggles, moulting and not fit to eat. I will give but two pence for the lot!'

'Make it four,' wheedled the cheapjack.

'Two!' cried the farmer, 'and not a half-penny more!'

Mother Farthing looked at her landlord, looked at the cheapjack, looked at the basket of hens. She thought of the long road home and the ache she had in her shoulder.

'Three pence,' she said, knowing the hens were worth more.

'Two pence,' repeated the farmer. 'Take it or leave it, old woman.'

'I'll take it,' sighed Mother Farthing and held out her hand for the coins.

'Hold hard!' said a voice as chill as a frosty morning. 'Two pence for the hens alone. A silver crown for the basket to carry them in.'

'What!' roared the farmer. 'Pay a silver crown for that tattered, battered old basket? Not I! No, indeed, not I!'

'Then the basket belongs to the old woman still,' said the little green magic man, 'and you must manage without it.'

'We'll see about that!' said the farmer and stooped to pick up the hamper.

With a crash and a crack the lid was flung back and six flapping hens were loose in the market square.

In a moment all was confusion. Dogs barked, boys larked. They raced and they chased, they shouted and clouted. Babies were crying and feathers were flying. Ducking and clucking, the hens ran about the street.

The lean man, the mean man, the man without a smile ran this way and that way, trying to catch them.

> 'Satchkin Patchkin!
> Your hens you shall not snatchkin!
> Satchkin Patchkin!
> Your hens you shall not snatch!'

sang the mocking voice of the little green magic man.

Mother Farthing picked up the empty hamper and hoisted it up on her shoulder. It lay there as light as a paper poke and the ache was no ache at all.

The farmer flung down a silver crown on the cobblestones at her feet. 'Leave the basket!' he cried and scurried away, for the cheapjack had captured a hen.

With a smile the old woman picked up the coin and put it safely away. Then she turned and went quickly out of the market place. All the way home she thought she heard singing like little bells ringing and she knew the words of the song.

'My name is Satchkin Patchkin and I live, like a leaf, in the apple tree.'

4

THE BROWN EGG
WILL NOT HATCH

ONCE UPON a time there was a little green magic man. His name was Satchkin Patchkin and he lived, like a leaf in an apple tree.

The apple tree grew by the hedge at the bottom of a long, untidy garden. At the other end of the long, untidy garden was the small, untidy cottage where Mother Farthing lived. Its windows were cracked, its doors hung askew, but the thatch on its tip-tilted roof was new. So were the curtains that hung in the old woman's bedroom.

'It will take more than two pence and a silver crown to mend the doors and windows,' Mother Farthing said. So she went to the market and bought a remnant of bright-coloured cloth to hang at her broken windows.

Out in the garden the wind was loosening the tangled grasses and blowing the blossoms down from the apple tree. As the old woman stood looking up at her newly-hung curtains a drift of white feathers swirled about her feet.

She stooped and collected a few, smoothing them in her fingers.

'My hens have left enough feathers behind to make a cloak for the little green magic man,' she thought and began to search for more.

About the wild and weedy garden she went, stumbling among the tumbled grasses, briar and bramble snatching and catching her skirts.

At last her pocket was full of feathers, downy and brown and white and light and a few little ones as black as night.

All the long morning the old woman sat at her scrubbed kitchen table sorting and stitching the softly curling feathers, fashioning a cloak for Satchkin Patchkin.

'I stitch and I sew but the cloak does not grow,' she sighed as the afternoon sun came slanting past the window. 'My old hands are too rough for such delicate stuff and my fingers are clumsy as thumbs.'

She finished the cloak as the sun slipped down behind the hill and a little shivering wind leapt up in the garden.

Opening the creaking, heavy and leaking, ill-fitting kitchen door, Mother Farthing called in a tired voice:

> 'Satchkin Patchkin,
> Hear me lift the latchkin.
> Satchkin Patchkin,
> Hear me lift the latch.'

Like the sound of a silver bell came the clear reply: 'You have forgotten to throw the thimble into the jug.'

'It was not milk I wanted,' answered Mother Farthing. 'I have made you a cloak from the finest feathers my seven hens shed in the garden.'

'That was a kindly thought,' said the little green magic man and he landed, soft as thistledown, on the old woman's outstretched hand. 'Spring may be waking the daffodils, but the winter chill is still in the evening wind. I shall sleep as warm as a bird in my feathery cloak.'

He lifted the cloak and wrapped it about himself, over his shoulders and down his back, white and brown and speckled with black. Now he was warm as a nestling under its mother's wing.

'Blow me away,' he commanded and the old woman blew him off the palm of her hand. He drifted like a puff-ball into the twilight.

When he was gone Mother Farthing slowly closed the stiff and difficult door. Then she lighted a candle and took herself off to bed.

She woke the next morning to hear such a clucking and squawking, so much loud chicken-talking that she thought at first her room was full of hens. She sat up and saw it was not, she stood up and looked out of the window.

Halfway down the long, untidy garden, in a hollow stump by a bramble clump, the small black hen was sitting.

She was making so much noise that Mother Farthing hurried out to see what was the matter. Her bare feet loose in her unlaced shoes and her shawl flung over her nightgown, the old woman ran through the damp and dewy grass.

The hen cackled and clucked and sat cosily tucked in the moss-lined hollow tree. The old woman lifted her up and saw beneath her seven beautiful eggs. Six were as white and meek as milk and one as brown and sleek as silk.

Mother Farthing knew at once that this was the work of Satchkin Patchkin. He had gone by night in the moon's low light to the farm at the top of the hill.

He did not wake the farmer from his bed. He knew that the lean man, the mean man, the man without a smile, would not give him what he wanted. He went, instead, to the henhouse and whistled the eggs from under the broody hen, sending them bowling, merrily rolling down the hill to Mother Farthing's garden.

In due time the white eggs were hatched and six

yellow chicks with legs like sticks went cheeping and creeping through the tumbled grass. Yet still the black hen sat on the smooth brown egg and it did not hatch. The chicks grew stronger, their legs grew longer, they lost their sun-coloured down.

'Soon I shall have six fine young birds to take to market,' thought Mother Farthing as she fed them.

Yet still the black hen sat on the smooth brown egg and it did not hatch.

'There is something about this egg that is not quite right,' thought Mother Farthing, taking it, shaking it, holding it up to the light. 'I do believe it has a spell on it.'

Hardly had the thought come into her head when she heard the silvery sound of the little green magic man singing:

> 'Satchkin Patchkin,
> The brown egg will not hatchkin . . .
> Satchkin Patchkin,
> The brown egg will not hatch.'

'What use is it, then?' asked the old woman, looking about her to see if she could find Satchkin Patchkin.

Like the clink and chink of a spoon in a glass came the tinkling, clear reply.

'Take it and break it and make me a honey cake.'

Without another word the old woman turned and went quickly back to her cottage. The fire needed tending and while it was mending she fetched from the larder the bowl for mixing the cake.

Then she took the brown egg and struck it smartly with a knife. As the silken shell broke a great golden yolk fell heavily into the bowl. The old woman put the broken shell on the table and picked up a fork. With a click and a clack and no sign of a crack the two halves of the eggshell joined themselves together again. As soon as she lifted the new-formed egg Mother Farthing knew by its weight that the shell was not empty.

Once again the egg broke and a great, golden yolk slid down into the bowl. The old woman put the two halves of the shell gently on the table and they instantly joined themselves together again.

'Milk I have in plenty and eggs I have in plenty,' cried Mother Farthing. 'I will make not one but a whole batch of honey cakes and take them to the market to sell. When they are sold I may have enough gold to mend my broken windows. The best cake, though, I will keep for the little green magic man.'

It was almost night and a faint, star light was flickering in the sky when the old woman made her weary way down the long, untidy garden.

In a white cloth she carried the best of the honey cakes. Without saying a word she put the cloth on a flat stone under the tree and turned to go back to her cottage.

Behind her she heard the last trill of a bird and then, sweet and clear, the voice of the little green magic man.

'My name is Satchkin Patchkin and I live, like a leaf, in the apple tree.'

5

CLEAR THE BRAMBLE PATCH

ONCE UPON a time there was a little green magic man. His name was Satchkin Patchkin and he lived, like a leaf, in an apple tree.

The apple tree grew by the hedge at the bottom of a long, untidy garden. Its hedges were tangled, its plants had been strangled by tussocks and hassocks of wild, winding grass.

At the other end of the long, untidy garden was the cottage where Mother Farthing lived. Its door hung askew but its thatched roof was new and its windows had been repaired. The glass was not shattered, the lead was not battered, they rattled and clattered no more.

Mother Farthing had walked to the town with her basket of honey cakes and found a market for them. She bought with the money more flour and more honey and went home to start baking again.

Day after young spring day blew brightly away on the wings of the wind. Every morning the old woman trudged up the long hill towards the town and came back at noon with her basket empty. Every afternoon she spent making and baking the honey cakes for the morrow. So many she sold that she soon had the gold to pay for the new latticed windows.

'A few batches more will pay for a door,' she thought, counting the coins in her purse.

Now she began to take saffron cakes and gingerbread. Milk she had in plenty and eggs she had in plenty and she never forgot to thank the little green magic man. Every evening she went down the long, untidy garden to the apple tree with the best of the afternoon's baking. She was tired and she stumbled but she never once grumbled as she dragged through the tangled grass.

One day she was tripped by a bramble and slipped and all but fell to the ground.

'I will bake no cakes tomorrow,' she cried. 'Instead I will come and work in my wicked garden. It is time I made it as neat as the workmen are making my cottage.'

Bird-early next morning Mother Farthing went into the dew-drenched garden. With bill-hook and fork she soon set to work clearing a path to the apple tree.

As she forked up the twigs and the rosemary sprigs and the grass she had hacked away, the old woman's hand was snatched and scratched by a straggling blackberry shoot.

Throwing the forkful of rubbish on to the heap she was making, she turned to cut back the blackberry bush. Then she saw, with surprise, that, juicy and plump, all over the clump, fine blackberries were growing.

'Here's a find!' she cried. 'I must fetch a basin at once and gather the fruit before it grows too ripe.'

She was pricked, she was scratched, her stockings were snatched, but the old woman did not care, for the fruit was sweet and good. Soon the basin was filled and she had to fetch out a bowl. The bowl was almost full by the time the great tangled bramble had been stripped clean.

Mother Farthing was putting the last sweet berry into her mouth to reward herself for her labours when she heard the sound of a horse coming down the hill. Louder and louder grew the hoof-beats, cli-clippety clop till they came to a stop at the old woman's garden gate.

In a moment a man came round by the cottage, a riding crop in his hand. He was a lean man, a mean man, a man without a smile – the old woman's land-lord come to collect his rent.

Mother Farthing fetched out the gold from the cakes she had sold and paid the farmer his due. As he counted the coins his eye fell on the bowl of black-berries the old woman had left on the step.

'That's a fine bowl of fruit, old woman,' he said. 'You must have gone far for those.'

'Not far, sir,' said the old woman, dropping a curtsey. 'They all came from this old garden.'

'Indeed!' cried the farmer. 'Then they are mine, old woman. You have not tended the garden this many a day. The land is mine and what grows on it wild is mine. You had better take dish and basket and fetch me the rest of the fruit.'

With that he took up the bowl of berries and hurried away.

Mother Farthing sighed and looked at the garden. It was long, it was wide and down either side was a tangle of thorn that served for a hedge. The brambles had scrambled and twisted and rambled everywhere. To gather all the berries for the farmer was a task that was frightful and prickly and spiteful and would take the old woman all day.

'If it is to be done it had best be begun,' she said and went to find a basket.

Before she started picking, however, she put a few of the biggest berries from the basin on the table into a little dish, with sugar and cream.

Then she went to the door and called:

> 'Satchkin Patchkin,
> Hear me lift the latchkin . . .
> Satchkin Patchkin,
> Hear me lift the latch!'

Like the sound of a far-off bell came the sweet reply: 'You have forgotten to throw the thimble into the jug.'

'It was not milk I wanted,' said Mother Farthing. 'I have no cake for you today, only a dish of berries.'

'Berries will do very well,' said the little green magic man and leapt on to the table to eat them.

Mother Farthing took up the basket and went out to the brambly garden.

Far into the afternoon the old woman worked. She was scratched, she was pricked, she was snatched, she was nicked. Her black skirt was dragged and her stockings were snagged and the pins were pulled out of her hair.

At last, with a sigh, she sat wearily down on a fallen tree.

'I never knew there were so many blackberries in my garden,' she said, pushing the hair from her eyes.

'Yet you worked with a will and cheerfully still to clear them away this morning,' said the cool voice of Satchkin Patchkin.

Light as a butterfly, green as a leaf, he leapt on to the old woman's purple-stained hand.

'I was doing it for myself,' said Mother Farthing.

'Now I do it because I must. My landlord wants the berries.'

'Then he shall have them,' laughed the little green magic man and began to sing:

> 'Satchkin Patchkin,
> Clear the bramble patchkin . . .
> Satchkin Patchkin . . .
> Clear the bramble patch!'

Twisting and bending and tearing and rending, the blackberry bushes pulled themselves out of the ground. Loosely and juicily, berries flew into the air.

Over the sun-sleepy fields they went, meadow and fallow, hillock and hollow, in a purple, glistening cloud. They fell on the farmhouse like hailstones, staining the windows and smearing the doors and dropping straight down the chimneys.

As for the bushes, they tumbled themselves over the hedge, roots ripped, twigs stripped and fell into the corn.

The farmer's wife had the fright of her life and ran into the farmyard, screaming. The lean, mean man himself went slithering, slipping, tumbling and tipping into a great heap of berries.

Mother Farthing picked up her basket and turned towards her cottage.

All about her the evening air was sweet with singing.

'My name is Satchkin Patchkin and I live, like a leaf, in the apple tree.'

6

SPREAD YOUR SHAWL
AND CATCH

ONCE UPON a time there was a little green magic man. His name was Satchkin Patchkin and he lived, like a leaf, in an apple tree.

The apple tree grew by the hedge at the bottom of a long, untidy garden. A tangle of brambles no longer scrambled the length and breadth of the garden but the grass was not cut, the earth was not levelled, it was lumpy and bumpy and torn and dishevelled.

At the other end of the garden stood the small cottage where Mother Farthing lived. Its curtains, its thatch and its windows were new but its worm-eaten doors still hung sadly askew.

In the chilly, bird-busy morning Mother Farthing rose and set about her baking. As she took a fresh batch of honey cakes from the oven she remembered the basin of blackberries she had gathered the day before.

'There are not berries enough to make tarts to sell

in the market,' she thought, 'so I will make a pie for myself and the little green magic man.'

When the pie was cool Mother Farthing cut a generous slice and topped it with cream. Then she went to the door and called:

'Satchkin Patchkin,
Hear me lift the latchkin . . .
Satchkin Patchkin,
Hear me lift the latch.'

'You have forgotten to throw the thimble into the jug,' came the calm, clear answer.

'It was not milk I wanted,' said the old woman. 'I have cut you a slice of blackberry pie.'

'So I see,' said the little green magic man, leaping light to the table. 'A generous slice, it looks juicy and nice.'

'It should have been blackberry and apple,' the old woman said, thinking of the hard, green apples on her tree, 'but the fruit is nowhere near ripe.'

'It will be ripe tomorrow,' said Satchkin Patchkin. 'Make me another pie, then.'

'I have no more berries,' Mother Farthing told him, 'but I will search the lane and see what I can find.'

'Do not put yourself to the trouble,' Satchkin Patchkin said. 'Wash out the basin with water from the spring, leave it on your windowsill tonight and I will fill it for you.'

The old woman did as she was bid and next morning she found the basin full to the brim with shining blackberries.

'When I return from the market,' she said, 'I will gather the fruit from the apple tree and make apple and blackberry pie.'

She took up the basket of cakes she had baked the day before and set off for the town. There was never a moment of doubt in her mind, for the little green magic man had said she would find the apples were ripe.

Now the apple had been set, long ago, thin and shivering and little and low, by the hedge at the end of the garden. As it grew it was blown and now it had grown away from the wind and leaned across the hedge. Most of its crop of small apples would drop into the field beyond.

The old woman's landlord never troubled about the apples. Hard they had been and bitter and green, and they did not improve with keeping.

In the bustling town the old woman sat down in her usual place in the square. She had no need to cry her wares for her customers knew her already. All her cakes were soon sold, she changed pence into gold and began the long walk home.

As she reached the top of the hill she saw, in the lane before her, a man upon a horse. It was the farmer, her landlord, riding to look at his land.

He turned his horse into the field by the old woman's cottage. He rode round the edge to make sure that the hedge would hold his new flock of sheep.

When he came to the place where the apple tree grew, he saw, with surprise, that it was laden with fruit. The farmer reached up and plucked an apple from the end of a bending bough. It was ripe, it was mellow, its skin was pale yellow, it was crisp, it was sweet.

'Why have I never noticed this tree before?' mused the farmer, taking another bite of the apple. 'It bears excellent fruit. It is well laden, too – enough to last me the winter. I will send my men with baskets directly, to gather this fine crop of apples.'

He rode out of the field and into the lane just as the old woman reached her garden gate. She dropped him a curtsey but he said not a word as he passed. He was a lean man, a mean man, a man without a smile, and cared nothing for courtesy.

Mother Farthing went into her cottage and put down her basket. When she had rested a little, she drank a mug of milk and ate some bread and cheese. Then she took up the basket again and went into the garden.

Hardly had she taken the first smooth apple from the tree when she heard the rattle and clatter of a cart in the lane. In a moment there were men in the field beyond the hedge. They were carrying baskets and rough pointed ladders and coming towards the tree.

The old woman knew at once what they were

after. She cried out to the little green magic man she knew was among the leaves:

'Satchkin Patchkin!
My apples they will snatchkin!
Satchkin Patchkin,
My apples they will snatch!'

Then she began to gather the fruit as fast as she could, dropping and plopping it into the basket at her feet, quite forgetting that apples misused will become apples bruised.

As the men drew nearer the old woman could hear them arguing among themselves.

' 'Tis the old woman's tree,' said one. 'We've no right to touch it.'

' 'Tis leaning over the hedge,' said another. 'If the fruit should drop it will drop into the field.'

By this time they had reached the tree and were pushing the awkward, pointed ladder into the branches. The farmer came striding after them, sour-faced to find them so slow.

'Make haste, you laggards!' he cried. 'I want all the fruit picked by sundown.'

Stretching and snatching and reaching and catching, Mother Farthing was gathering her apples as fast as she could.

Then, from among the leaves above her, came a sound like the ringing of far-off silver bells.

'Satchkin Patchkin!
Spread your shawl and catchkin . . .
Satchkin Patchkin!
Spread your shawl and catch.'

Mother Farthing snatched up her shawl from the log where she had thrown it and spread it on the ground.

Shaking and quivering, every leaf shivering, the apple tree leaned slowly away from the hedge. Its branches were swung up and apples were flung up, high into the air.

Like great flakes of snow they fell, gentle and slow, and settled themselves on the shawl.

In the field the lean, mean farmer stood speechless. His men were struck dumb, their limbs had grown numb, they were stuck to the ground with fright.

Out of the trembling tree came the clear, sweet voice again.

'My name is Satchkin Patchkin and I live, like a leaf, in the apple tree.'

7

BAKE ANOTHER BATCH

ONCE UPON a time there was a little green magic man. His name was Satchkin Patchkin and he lived, like a leaf, in an apple tree.

The apple tree leaned away from the hedge at the bottom of a long and tidy garden. At the other end of the long and tidy garden stood the small, neat cottage where Mother Farthing lived. The thatch on its tip-tilted roof was new and its well-fitting doors had been painted blue. Its curtains were gay, its bright windows shone and all its neglected appearance was gone.

While the men were working on the cottage Mother Farthing was working in the garden. She weeded the pathways and trimmed the tall hedge and set out a border with stones at the edge. The rubbish was burned and the earth was new turned and nine rows of cabbages planted.

The old woman rose at daybreak to bake her cakes and pastries and took them fresh to the market. Such good luck she had with her wares that she bought a small donkey to carry the heavy basket.

When her cakes were all gone she rode merrily home and set to work in her garden.

'I will plant and sow and dig and hoe,' she said to herself, 'and next year I will have a stall in the market place and sell good green things from my garden along with my cakes and pastries.'

The old woman reckoned without her landlord, though. He was a lean man, a mean man, a man without a smile. He came riding by one morning as she was leading the donkey into the lane.

'What have you in your basket, old woman?' he asked.

The old woman dropped him a curtsey. 'Cakes and pastries, sir,' she answered, folding back the snowy cloth for him to see.

The farmer leaned down and took out a honey cake, stuffing it hungrily into his eager mouth.

Crumbs fell over his chin and on to his waistcoat. Flicking and licking his fingers, he said, 'I have come for your rent. If you have not enough to pay me I will take the donkey instead.'

Hastily the old woman began to fumble in her skirts for the pocket she wore at her waist.

'Here is the rent,' she said, speedily paying it out. She had no desire to lose her little donkey.

'It is hardly enough,' grumbled the farmer, counting the coins. 'You live here in comfort and pay me a miserable rent.'

Mother Farthing was about to say that the cottage had been a miserable cottage till she herself had set it to rights, but she thought better of it and held her tongue.

'You shall make me a gift,' the lean, mean man went on. 'A score of your cakes and pastries will do for a start.'

With a sigh Mother Farthing went indoors to fetch a platter. She piled it with cakes and pastries and wrapped a clean cloth about it.

'My customers in the market will go short, I fear, this morning,' she said.

'Bake another batch, then,' said the farmer and taking the platter rode quickly away.

The next day the old woman rose before dawn and set to work in her spotless kitchen, mixing and making and busily baking her delicious cakes and pies. Milk she had in plenty and eggs she had in plenty and a basin of berries fresh on her sill every day. She made cakes with honey, all sticky and nice, she used ginger and saffron and currants and spice and the best of her baking she saved every day for the little green magic man.

When the cooking was done, the kitchen cleaned and the basket packed, Mother Farthing made herself a breakfast of bread and milk and went out to see to the donkey.

She was leading him into the lane when the land-lord came riding by.

'My wife was well pleased with your gift, old woman,' he said. 'She hopes you will send her another score today.'

The old woman sighed and went indoors for a platter. She knew that she dare not refuse the farmer's request for fear he would turn her out of her little cottage.

'My customers will have to go short again today,' she said as she took the cakes and pies from the basket.

'You must bake another batch, then,' said the farmer and he took the platter and rode quickly away.

Sadly the old woman went back to the cottage and prepared for cooking again. She creamed and she iced, she sugared and spiced and she sighed all the while she worked.

The next day and the next the farmer came for a score of the old woman's cakes. The next day and the next she had to return to her cottage and bake another batch to fill her basket. The smell in her kitchen was spicy and nice but she did not like having to do her work twice.

On the fourth day, when Mother Farthing returned from the market with fresh supplies of flour and sugar and honey, she sat down to count the coins in her purse and found she had less than enough to put aside for the rent.

'I must ask the advice of the little green magic man,' she said and went to the door to call him.

> 'Satchkin Patchkin,
> Hear me lift the latchkin . . .
> Satchkin Patchkin,
> Hear me lift the latch!'

Like the ring of a far-off silvery bell came the sweet, familiar answer.

'You have forgotten to throw the thimble into the milk jug.'

'It was not milk I wanted,' said the old woman and she told him why she had called.

'We will see what tomorrow will bring,' said Satchkin Patchkin and he drifted away in the sunlight like a rose petal blown by the wind.

The next day the farmer demanded the basketful of cakes. 'You shall give me my harvest supper, old woman,' he said, paying no heed to her protests. 'It will save my wife the trouble of making a feast.'

'But my customers, sir!' cried Mother Farthing. 'How shall I satisfy them, with no cakes at all today?'

The farmer laughed and snatched the basket from Mother Farthing's hands. 'Bake another batch, old woman,' he cried as he rode away. 'Bake another batch!'

From the sky overhead there came ringing, chill as winter rain stinging, the voice of the little green magic man:

> 'Satchkin Patchkin,
> Bake another batchkin . . .
> Satchkin Patchkin . . .
> Bake another batch!'

Pie, pasty and cake began quickly to make themselves in the old woman's kitchen. From jar and from tin, from jug and from bin the ingredients flew together. Wood piled on the fire, the flames grew higher and higher till the oven was good and hot. Then batch after batch of cakes slid into the oven, were cooked and came out again. They rolled over the floor and out of the door and up the hill to the farm. With sackfuls of sugar and sackfuls of flour, with eggs, milk and honey, hour after hour, cakes made themselves and conveyed themselves to the home of the lean, mean man.

His windows were covered, his doorways were blocked, his yards were all filled and his barns were all stocked.

From over the meadows where the moon flung dark shadows came the sound of the midnight bell.

At once the old woman's kitchen set itself to rights. Her basket was packed and her table was stacked with wares for the morrow's market. There was more than enough of the magical stuff to pay her rent for a month, but the cakes in the farmyard high on the hill were turned into little round pebbles. Knobbly and hard they rolled over the yard and blocked every gateway and door.

Taking her candle the old woman climbed the narrow stairs to her bed. Down in the dark behind her she heard a familiar song.

'My name is Satchkin Patchkin and I live, like a leaf, in the apple tree.'

8

I HAVE MET MY MATCH

ONCE UPON a time there was a little green magic man. His name was Satchkin Patchkin and he lived, like a leaf, in an apple tree.

The apple tree leaned away from the hedge at the bottom of a long and tidy garden. It was autumn and the leaves, turning brown, had begun to drift down and litter the ground below.

At the other end of the long and tidy garden was the small, neat cottage where Mother Farthing lived. Smoke rose early in the air from her chimney and a lad from the village came at dawn to help her with her baking. Then he harnessed the little donkey to a bright new cart and drove into town to sell the cakes and pastries. They were gone, they were sold before they were cold and the lad went back for the old woman's second baking.

Mother Farthing had a fine new stove in her kitchen and a lock on her larder door. She kept to herself that the milk on the shelf and the one brown egg were the gifts of Satchkin Patchkin. She fetched in a basin of berries from the windowsill every morning, but the lad knew nothing of that. He thought the old woman must have a great store and he never questioned the locked larder door.

One sparkling day when the morning air was spiced with the smell of apple and blackberry pie, the old woman's landlord came riding down the hill. He was a lean man, a mean man, a man without a smile and he brought with him a man as lean and mean and mirthless as himself.

They left their horses to crop the sweet grass at Mother Farthing's gate and made their sour-faced way to the kitchen door.

Mother Farthing looked up from her mixing bowl and saw, at the door, her landlord. At his back, dressed all in black, stood a man with eyes like small grey pebbles.

'I am selling this cottage, old woman,' the landlord said. 'The lawyer has come to set a value upon it.'

With a cry of dismay Mother Farthing dropped her fork. A spatter of batter splashed down on the clean scrubbed floor.

Lawyer and landlord tramped all over the cottage,

poking and prying and peering and spying and
trying to work out its worth. They saw that the doors
had been painted blue and the thatch on the tip-
tilted roof was new, the windows were bright and
the doorstep was white and the grates all freshly
black-leaded.

They walked the long length of the garden and marked out and measured the plot. They examined the border with stones at the edge and noted the height of the trimmed, tidy hedge. It was all neat and nice, they agreed on a price and rode away to the town.

As soon as they had gone the old woman went to her kitchen door and cried out for the little green magic man:

> 'Satchkin Patchkin!
> Hear me lift the latchkin . . .
> Satchkin Patchkin,
> Hear me lift the latch!'

Like a droplet of water fresh from the spring the familiar voice replied:

'You have forgotten to throw the thimble into the jug.'

'It was not milk I wanted,' said the old woman and she told him her tale of woe.

'This far we have come and this much we have done,' said the little green magic man, looking round at the spotless kitchen. 'You had a talent and I had a spell, together you used them wisely and well. I promise your efforts shall not be wasted, Mother.'

Frail as a feather he drifted into the sunlight and the old woman saw and heard him no more that day.

In the night, by the light of a moon low and bright, Satchkin Patchkin set off up the hill. By hawthorn and oak like a puff of grey smoke he went, with the wind at his heels.

In the beamy, dreaming farmhouse the old woman's landlord lay snoring, deep in his feather bed. Beside him, round as a dumpling, his wife smiled in her sleep.

Into the farmer's dreams came a whispering like the sighing of summer leaves. 'Let the old woman have her cottage,' it said. 'Let her buy it herself.'

The farmer mumbled and snorted and grumbled and tried to shake off the dream.

Pale as a moth on the pillow, the little green magic man spoke again and again in the mean man's listening ear.

'Let the old woman have her cottage. Let her buy it herself.'

With a snort and a snore that was more like a roar the farmer sat up in bed.

'She shall not have it!' he shouted, waking his wife. 'I will ride to the town and settle the sale tomorrow.'

As soon as the ham and the strawberry jam of breakfast were cleared away, the farmer saddled his horse and rode into the lane.

There, no more than a yard or so from the gate, the horse stood still.

The farmer urged him on but he seemed not to hear. Again and again he jerked at the rein, but the horse refused to move. So still and firm he stood that he seemed to be turned to stone.

The lean man, the mean man was raving and ranting and puffing and panting, prodding and flicking and whipping and kicking in vain. The horse neither felt him nor heard him. He was under the spell of the little green magic man.

At last the farmer gave up and made to dismount, but his feet were held fast in the stirrups. Try as he might, he could not leave his horse.

He called to his men to help him. From the barns, from the fields, they came running, but they could not set him free. They pushed, pulled and jerked. Roughly, rudely they worked, secretly glad at his plight. He was bruised, he was battered, his clothes torn and tattered, but he could not get down from his horse.

The bright blue day grew dull and grey and a chill

wind blew with rain on its whistling breath. The farmer's men hastened away to the tasks they had left half-done.

The lean man, the mean man, the man without a smile, sat slumped on his cold stone horse, his wet hair wisped on his brow.

Sharp as the rain he heard once again the sting of an icy voice.

'Let the old woman have her cottage. Let her buy it herself.'

Wearily now the farmer raised his head. On the tip of his horse's left ear stood a little green magic man.

The farmer knew that he was beaten. His voice, when he spoke, was no more than a croak and the words that he uttered were, surely, not his own.

> 'Satchkin Patchkin,
> I have met my matchkin . . .
> Satchkin Patchkin,
> I have met my match.'

At once the horse shivered and trembled and quivered and came to life again. The farmer, still fast in the stirrups, turned him towards the town and the pebble-eyed lawyer.

One agreement was torn up, a new one was drawn up and the cottage was sold, for a handful of gold, to Mother Farthing herself. As the farmer leaned from his horse and put his name to the parchment, he felt his feet freed from the stirrups. He rode back to the farm on the hill and went nevermore to Mother Farthing's cottage.

The wind and the rain came again and again to wash the blue and gold from the autumn days. As the last of the leaves was torn from the trembling tree, old Mother Farthing, sitting close to her cheerful fire, heard for the last time the sweet, clear voice of the little green magic man.

'My name is Satchkin Patchkin and I drift, like a leaf, from the apple tree.'

Some other Young Puffins

ANNA, GRANDPA AND THE BIG STORM
Carla Stevens

Anna is just as determined as her usually grumpy Grandpa that she should get to school. It's the final of the spelling competition and she wants to be there. But as they struggle through the snow while the blizzard grows stronger and stronger, Anna begins to wonder whether they will ever get there. And when their train becomes snowbound, she begins to wonder whether they will ever get home again!

THE SNOW KITTEN
Nina Warner Hooke

Bewildered and hungry, the kitten wandered round the village hopelessly seeking food and shelter until it seemed as if his sad little life would end without ever having properly begun. But the children cared, and tried to work a miracle in time for Christmas

RETURN TO OZ
Alistair Hedley

A thrilling new Oz adventure, based on the photoplay by Walter Murch and Gill Dennis. Dorothy Gale finds herself in the magical land of Oz, but when she reaches her beloved Emerald City, she's in for a shock – for the people have been turned to Stone and Oz has been conquered by the wicked Nome King!

THE CONKER AS HARD AS A DIAMOND
Chris Powling

Last conker season Little Alpesh lost every single game! That's why he's determined this year's going to be different. This year he's going to win, and he won't stop until he's Conker Champion of the Universe. The trouble is, only a conker as hard as a diamond will make it possible – and where on earth will he find one?

MR MAJEIKA
Humphrey Carpenter

There was no denying it – a genuine magic carpet had just flown in through the classroom window in front of their very eyes. And what's more, Class Three's new teacher was sitting on it! This is just the beginning of the most extraordinary and hilarious school term ever.

BRIGHT-EYE
Alison Morgan

When her father brings home a wild duck's egg from the field he has ploughed, Amanda knows exactly what she's going to do; with a little help from Millie the speckled bantam, she's going to make sure this egg hatches out into a beautiful fluffy little duckling.

TALES FROM THE WIND IN THE WILLOWS
Kenneth Grahame

Mole thought life along the riverbank might be a little dull, but he couldn't have been more wrong. There were all sorts of animals living in and by the river, and one in particular who was anything *but* dull – Mr Toad. A new edition of this classic story about Mole, Water Rat, Badger and Toad, illustrated by Margaret Gordon and especially abridged for younger readers.

RAGDOLLY ANNA
Jean Kenward

Although she's only made from a morsel of this and a tatter of that, Ragdolly Anna is a very special doll. And within hours of beginning to live with the Little Dressmaker, the White Cat and Dummy, she embarks on some hair-raising adventures.

DUCK BOY
Christobel Mattingley

The holiday at Mrs Perry's farm doesn't start very well for Adam. His brother and sister don't want to spend any time with him, they say he's too young. At first he's bored and lonely, but then he discovers the creek and meets two ducks who need some help. Every year their eggs are stolen by rats or foxes, so Adam strikes a bargain with them: he'll help guard their nest if they'll let him learn to swim in their creek.

WORZEL GUMMIDGE AT THE FAIR

Keith Waterhouse and Willis Hall

Here he is again – the scatty Worzel Gummidge – neglecting his crow-scaring and trying to win back Aunt Sally from a fairground Strong Man. But the path of true love isn't easy for Worzel – especially when he meets another pretty scarecrow . . . This book has been specially written to allow younger readers to share in the hilarious adventures of the rascally scarecrow.

THE TELEVISION ADVENTURES OF SUPER GRAN
MORE TELEVISION ADVENTURE OF SUPER GRAN

Forrest Wilson

Since the day she was hit by a strange blue beam, Granny Smith has been Super Gran, a remarkable old lady with extraordinary powers of strength, speed and sight. In these two books, which have been filmed for television, her adventures include jewel-thieves, robots, cup-ties, clocks, golfers and dognappers.

CHRIS AND THE DRAGON

Fay Sampson

Chris is always in trouble of one kind or another, but does try extra hard to be good when he is chosen to play Joseph in the school nativity play. This hilarious story ends with a glorious celebration of the Chinese New Year.

THE RAILWAY CAT
THE RAILWAY CAT AND DIGBY
THE RAILWAY CAT'S SECRET
Phyllis Arkle

Stories about Alfie the Railway Cat and his sworn enemy Hack the porter in which Alfie tries to win over Hack by various means, with often hilarious results.

THE GHOST AT No. 13
Gyles Brandreth

Hamlet Brown's sister Susan is just too perfect. Everything she does is praised and Hamlet is in despair – until the ghost comes to stay for a holiday and helps him find an exciting idea for his school project.

ON THE NIGHT WATCH
Hannah Cole

A group of children and their parents occupy their tiny school in an effort to prevent its closure.

DINNER LADIES DON'T COUNT
Bernard Ashley

Two stories set in a school. Jason has to prove he didn't take Donna's birthday cards, and Linda tells a lie about why she can't go on the school outing

MOULDY'S ORPHAN
Gillian Avery

Mouldy dreams of adopting an orphan, but when she brings one home to her crowded cottage, Mum and Dad aren't pleased at all.

THE TALE OF GREYFRIARS BOBBY
Virginia Derwent

A specially retold version for younger readers of the true story of a scruffy Skye terrier who was faithful to his master even in death.